Twinkle
and the
Fairy Cake Mess

by Katharine Holabird • Illustrated by Sarah Warburton

Ready-to-Read

Simon Spotlight
New York   London   Toronto   Sydney   New Delhi

SIMON SPOTLIGHT
An imprint of Simon & Schuster Children's Publishing Division
1230 Avenue of the Americas, New York, New York 10020
This Simon Spotlight edition December 2020
Text copyright © 2020 by Katharine Holabird
Illustrations copyright © 2020 by Sarah Warburton
Illustrations by Cherie Zamazing
SIMON SPOTLIGHT, READY-TO-READ, and colophon are registered
trademarks of Simon & Schuster, Inc.
For information about special discounts for bulk purchases, please
contact Simon & Schuster Special Sales at 1-866-506-1949 or
business@simonandschuster.com.
Manufactured in the United States of America 1020 LAK
10 9 8 7 6 5 4 3 2 1
Library of Congress Cataloging-in-Publication Data
Names: Holabird, Katharine, author. I Warburton, Sarah, illustrator. Title:
Twinkle and the fairy cake mess / by Katharine Holabird ; illustrated by Sarah
Warburton. Description: Simon Spotlight edition. I New York : Simon Spotlight,
2020. I Series: Twinkle I Audience: Ages 5-7. I Audience: Grades K-1. I Summary:
Twinkle's attempts to bake a cake get messier and messier until she realizes
the ingredient she needs is help from her friends. Identifiers: LCCN 2020021343
I ISBN 9781534486201 (paperback) I ISBN 9781534486218 (hardcover) I ISBN
9781534486225 (ebook) Subjects: CYAC: Fairies—Fiction. I Baking—Fiction. I
Friendship—Fiction. Classification: LCC PZ7.H689 Twj 2020 I DDC [E]—dc23 LC
record available at https://lccn.loc.gov/2020021343

Twinkle was a pink fairy.
Her wings glowed
when she was happy
or excited.
They glowed a lot!

Twinkle was so happy to be
in fairy school.
Twinkle loved learning her spells.

Sometimes they worked.
And sometimes they did not.
But she always tried.

Today was a very special day.
All the fairies at
The Fairy School of Magic and Music
were going to a picnic!
There would be music!
There would be dancing!
There would be treats
and pinkberry tea!

Each fairy was to make
something special and bring it
to the picnic.
What should Twinkle make?
Twinkle spun around and thought.
And thought some more.

Then she had an idea!
Her fairy wings glowed.
All the fairies loved fairy cake.

They loved fairy cake
with lots of pink frosting.
Twinkle would bake a cake
for the picnic!

Twinkle ran to the kitchen.
She put on a sparkly apron.
She set out sugar and eggs and milk.

Oh no!

"Fiddlesticks!" she cried.

"Ooops. I forgot how to bake a cake!"

"I will try a spell," said Twinkle.
She waved her fairy wand.
"Abracadabra! Fiddle dee fee!
Let's bake a special cake
for a picnic with tea!"

Poof!
Oh no!
Twinkle's wand bumped the eggs.
Crack! Splat!
What a mess!

"I can fix this mess," said Twinkle.
"I just need to try again."
She closed her eyes.
"Abracadabra! Fiddle tee tee!
Put these cracked eggs
where no one can see!"

Oh no.
The eggs were still a mess.
And now Twinkle's spell knocked over
the cup of milk, too.

"Fairies never give up," said Twinkle.
"I just need to try harder."
Twinkle held up her wand.
She waved it over her head.

Swoosh!
Bump!
She spilled all the sugar.
It was sweet, but it was a mess.

"Oh dear," cried Twinkle.
"I can't bake a cake.
And now I have made a very big mess."
Twinkle sat down on the floor.
She took a deep breath in.
She let out the air.

"Oh, that feels better," Twinkle said.
So she took another deep breath in,
and let out the air.
Twinkle breathed deeply
until she felt strong.
Then she stood up and grandly waved
her wand.
"Abracadabra! Fiddle dee dee!
I need someone to come help me!"

Ding-dong!

Pippa and Lulu were at the door.

"I'm so glad you're both here,"
said Twinkle.

"I need some magic help."

"We can help you!" said Pippa.
"When a friend needs help,
we always help," said Lulu.

Twinkle showed Pippa and Lulu
the kitchen.
"I wanted to bake a cake
for the fairy picnic," she said.
"But my spells got sillier and sillier,
and I made a big mess!"
"Don't worry, Twinks,
we'll help you bake a cake!"
said Pippa.
"We love baking!" said Lulu.
"But first we'll help you clean up."

Twinkle gave her friends
sparkly aprons.
Pippa held up her wand.
"Abracadabra! Fiddle dee foo!
A friend is someone
who will always help you!"

"Pippa!" cried Twinkle. "You did it!"
The sugar went back in the bowl.
The milk went back in the cup.
The eggs went back in the carton.

Pippa smiled. "Now let's bake a cake!"
Together the fairies sorted and mixed
and put the cake in the oven to bake.

FLOUR

Then Twinkle and her friends
made pink frosting.
They each tasted a little,
just to make sure it was good.
Then they covered the cake
with heaps of pink frosting.

"We need some sparkles!" said Twinkle.
She put sprinkles on top.
"There!" she said.
"Oh, it looks so yummy!" said Lulu.
"Everyone at the picnic will
love it!"

"We made a super delicious
fairy cake!" said Twinkle.
"Yes," said Pippa. "We did it together.
And everything is better
when you do it with friends!"

Twinkle smiled. "It is!" she agreed.
"We will always help you
when you ask for help," said Pippa.
Lulu nodded. "That is what friends do."
"And I will always help too,
whenever you need me," said Twinkle.
"Abracadabra! Fiddle tee fee!
Pippa and Lulu will always
be best friends to me!"

But Twinkle waved her wand
a little too wide and stuck it
in the cake. Oh no!
Lulu gave Twinkle a big hug.

"Maybe you need to work
on your spells," said Pippa.
"But we will be your friends
even when your spells make a mess!"

Twinkle, Pippa, and Lulu flew
to the picnic.
They placed their cake on a table
filled with treats.
Twinkle and her friends spent
the rest of the day playing games
and enjoying all the yummy food.
And everyone agreed that the
yummiest thing of all was
the fairy friends' perfectly pink
fairy cake.